The Downstairs Bears

The Upstairs Downstairs Bears at Christmas

by Carol Lawson

Heinemann • London

For
Chris

First published in Great Britain 1997
by W H Books Ltd
an imprint of Reed International Books Limited
Michelin House, 81 Fulham Road, London SW3 6RB
Auckland and Melbourne
Licensed by Gresham Licensing Ltd

0 434 801046
Printed in Belgium by Proost

Freddy

Henry

Alice

Henrietta

Baby Arthur

Number 49
Theodore Square

Kitty

Barker

Winston

Flora Mardle

Mrs Bumble

Polly

Nanny Maybold

It was still dark when the postman rang the bell of number 49 Theodore Square, home of the Bosworth family. Flora Mardle the parlour maid woke with a start. Christmas Eve! Shivering, she jumped out of bed, dressed quickly and ran down the two flights of stone stairs to collect the mail.

Polly the little kitchen maid and Winston the footman were already busy about the house.

Downstairs in the kitchen,
Mrs Bumble the cook was preparing breakfast
for the whole household.

Barker the butler took the letters from Flora and strode down the hallway. In the breakfast room the lamps were lit and the table laid ready for the Upstairs Bears.

Freddy Bosworth unfolded his newspaper and sniffed appreciatively. “Mmm, kippers!” he said, “my favourite!” Henrietta, his wife, was making a list. “However will I get everything done?” she said. “Will you order the tree, Freddy? And Kitty, you can help Winston with the holly.” Kitty sighed and put that day’s letter from her fiancé, Binkie Bartholomew, into her pocket.

Upstairs in the nursery, the younger Bosworth bears were having their breakfast. Nanny Maybold was feeding Baby Arthur while Alice and Henry finished their porridge.

The little bears were excited.
This morning they were going shopping with Nanny and Flora, and there was the promise of a special treat.
"I'll expect best behaviour please," said Nanny.
"Remember, polite bears are welcome bears, especially in shops."

When Nanny and Flora had bought all the things on the list, Nanny said, "We have just one more shop to visit before we go home for lunch."

"What kind of shop...?" asked Henry.

"...and what are we going to buy there?" asked Alice.

"Patience is a virtue," said Nanny Maybold. "Wait and see."

Holding tightly onto Flora, the twins followed Nanny round a corner and found themselves in front of the biggest shop they had ever seen!

Wide-eyed they went through the huge swing doors.

Suddenly a voice said, "This way if you please."
Alice turned to see a bear in a beautiful fairy costume.
She was beckoning them to follow her.
Nanny straightened Henry's scarf and
smoothed Alice's coat.
"Off you go," she said, "and remember,
tidy bears are welcome bears."
"Where is the fairy taking us?" whispered Henry to Alice.
"I don't know, but let's follow her and see," said Alice.

At the end of a long sparkly corridor the twins
caught sight of a large figure in a red robe.
"It's Father Christmas!" they gasped.

Alice didn't want to leave the toy department but Nanny said they were needed at home so she had to wave goodbye to the fairy and follow the others out into the street.

On the way back Flora bought some hot chestnuts and Henry and Alice skipped along chattering and munching.

After lunch, Nanny sent the twins downstairs to the kitchen with Flora while Baby Arthur had his afternoon rest.

"Come in, come in, my dears," called Mrs Bumble when she saw Alice and Henry.

She put the pudding basin on the kitchen table, gave them a large wooden spoon and set them to work.

"You can never give a pudding too much stirring!" said Mrs Bumble.

"And don't forget to make a wish."

The little bears were stirring and wishing
when the outside door suddenly flew open
and in came Winston with
a rush of cold air and snowflakes.

"Snow!" cried Henry and Alice,
"that's just what we were wishing for!"

Dressed in their warmest clothes,
the bears set off for the park.

The twins were having fun playing in the snow when they heard a faint cry. Looking round they saw a small figure waving to them from the top of the hill. "Yoo-hoo! It's me, Binkie! I've got a brand new sledge and I'm going to try it out on this slope!"

Freddy looked up. " Don't you think it's a bit..." he began as the sledge zoomed down the hill. "...steep?" finished Freddy, shaking his head as Binkie and the sledge disappeared from view.

"Oh, oh, I can't stop!" shouted Binkie.

The twins were the first to reach the top of the ridge. They saw the upturned sledge but there was no sign of Binkie. "Where can he be?" said Henry. Suddenly they heard a very strange growly sound.

"I think it's coming from that snowbear," said Henry nervously. "Come on, let's take a look," said Alice. At that moment the snowbear shook itself violently. "It's Binkie!" cried the twins. "That's enough sledging for me," he said. "Let's go home."

Down in the kitchen, Polly was struggling to make long garlands of holly and ivy. She was very glad when Kitty and the twins arrived back to help her.

Suddenly the doorbell rang.
Everyone came to lend a hand and the enormous tree
was carried into the sitting room.

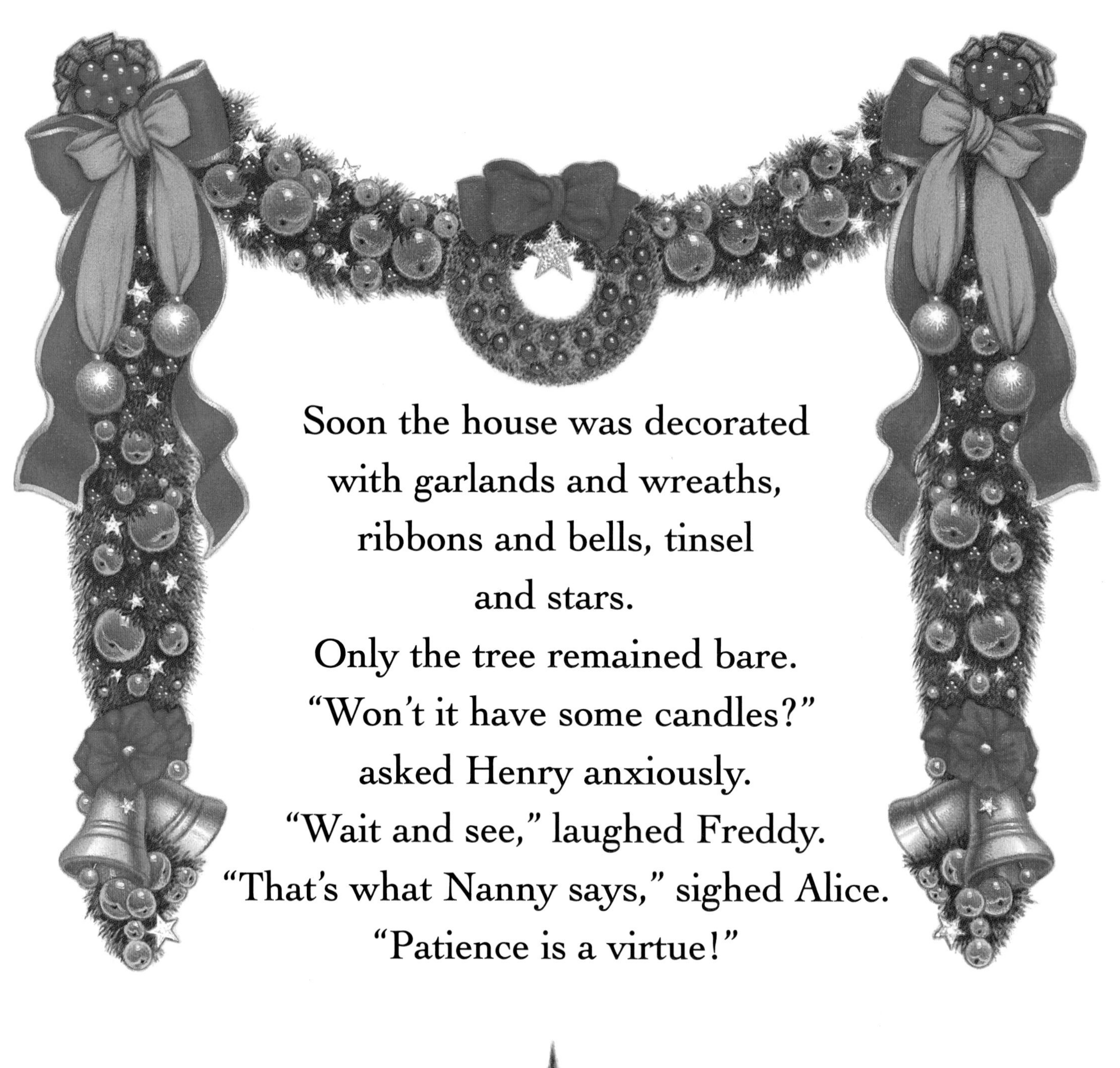

Soon the house was decorated
with garlands and wreaths,
ribbons and bells, tinsel
and stars.
Only the tree remained bare.
"Won't it have some candles?"
asked Henry anxiously.
"Wait and see," laughed Freddy.
"That's what Nanny says," sighed Alice.
"Patience is a virtue!"

The twins were on their way to bed when they
heard the sound of music drifting up from the street.
"Now I wonder what that might be?"
said Nanny Maybold.

She took Alice and Henry
and Baby Arthur
downstairs and
opened the
front door.

There stood all the Upstairs and Downstairs Bears
singing carols at the tops of their voices.
"...And now it really is time for bed,"
said Nanny as the carol singers came to the end of their
concert and made their way next door.

Soon the little bears were fast asleep and by midnight the lights at 49 Theodore Square were out and all was quiet and still.

Henry and Alice woke to feel something heavy
on their beds - their Christmas stockings!

By eight o'clock the Downstairs Bears
were already busy.
Mrs Bumble was in the kitchen preparing vegetables.
Winston was polishing the silver
and Flora was shaking out the best tablecloth for the
dining room table.
Polly was sent upstairs to help Nanny.

Soon it was time for Nanny to take the twins and
Baby Arthur down to the drawing room.
"Knock on the door, Alice dear, and see if they are
ready for us," said Nanny.

As the doors swung open, the little bears
stared in wonder.
The tree, so green and bare yesterday, was now
hung with garlands and stars that sparkled in the
light of a hundred candles.
And beneath the tree there were presents
for everyone.

"A warm bear is a happy bear," beamed Nanny Maybold, admiring her new shawl.

Freddy picked Alice up and held her high in the air.
"There is the rest of your present," he said.
"Can you reach it?"
"The Christmas Fairy!" cried Alice.
"She looks just like the fairy in the grotto!"
"Happy Christmas everyone!" said Henrietta.
"Happy Christmas," they all shouted in reply.

"Time for Christmas dinner,"
said Mrs Bumble.

When the pudding was finished and everyone
had congratulated Mrs Bumble on her cooking,
the fun really began.

In the drawing room the furniture was moved aside and the carpet rolled back. They played Musical Bears and Blind Bear's Buff, Pin the Tail on the Bear and Postbear's Knock until they were all quite out of breath.

As night drew in and the lamps were lit at 49 Theodore Square, the Upstairs and Downstairs Bears sat sleepily together around the dying embers of the fire.

The little bears had long since fallen asleep on the hearth rug. Henry and Baby Arthur's dreams were full of games and sledging and snowbears.

But Alice smiled happily in her sleep and dreamed only of the beautiful Christmas Fairy, the best Christmas present of all.

The Upstairs Bears